ADVENTURES OF

MAX

THE SCOTCH COMMANDER

KATHY RUTH (HALL) HAACK

CITIOFBOOKS, INC.

3736 Eubank NE Suite A1

Albuquerque, NM 87111-3579

www.citiofbooks.com

| Hotline: | 1 (877) 389-2759 |
| Fax: | 1 (505) 930-7244 |

Ordering Information:

Quantity sales. Special discounts are available on quantity purchases by corporations, associations, and others. For details, contact the publisher at the address above.

Printed in the United States of America.

| ISBN-13: | Softcover | 979-8-90124-242-1 |
| | eBook | 979-8-90124-243-8 |

Library of Congress Control Number: 2026908439

Table of Contents

Jamie and Brody Hall

DEDICATION

Brian Hall, my son
Jamie and Brody Hall, my grandsons
Bill E. Einsel, my brother
And **Sherman Mills**, Max's buddy
Who are all great dog lover

IN HONOR OF

All dog lovers, including dog trainers, dog groomers, Veterinarians, dog walkers dog authors and pet owners across the world

IN MEMORY OF

Randall W. Haack
(Max's Dad)

Paul L. Einsel
(Kathy's father)
Served in the Navy during WWII
Fought in a Navy destroyer ship in the Philippine Basin seas near Okinawa.

Jermiah Einsel
(Kathy's grandfather) Served in the Army World War I Fought on the Normandy Beaches against Hitler and his German Army.

Walter Haack
(Randy's father)
Served in the Army during WWII

AUTHORS PURPOSE

In this story, through the character of Max, I'm portraying that freedom and equality are worth fighting for even though sacrifices may have to be made. The values of honor, bravery and justice are enunciated.

In this case the rights and freedom of all dogs regardless of breed or birth location are protected and honored. Faith, hope and justice are restored in a free society.

(An Analogy that all people regardless of race, religion or creed deserve freedom and equality of life)

The story is written for teenagers to not only entertain them but to teach or encourage true values and morality taking place in real geological areas and some true historical events.

ACKNOWLEDGEMENTS AND CREDITS

Kathy Ruth (Hall) Haack
Author, artist of Max Starry Night painting, and photographer
Kathy's historical research materials include PBS-documented World War II films, the Great World Atlas, and Webster's Dictionary

Jamie Hall
Grandson of the author; creator of Max in the Scottish uniform image, Creator of Max with eye goggles in airplane

Pat Baily
Creator of the Bulldog and Submarine

Citi of Books
Publisher and printer

Derrick Hogan and Design Team
Illustrating Max's Three Generals, Max Flying a Spit Fire Plane, Battle Scenes, Heisler and cover (**Matthew Cross**)

Kathy Ruth (Hall) Haack

ABOUT THE AUTHOR
Kathy R. Haack

Kathy's love of animals was derived from growing up near her grandfather, Aquilla F. Burton's farm. The street was named after her grandfather, Burton Avenue located in Carney, Maryland.

The love of family and children are of paramount importance to Kathy. She had two children, Tracy (now deceased) and Brian who has three children that Kathy adores. Her personal goal is to promote happiness, harmony and peace within her family domain.

Kathy has been writing since her college days and painting since she was fifteen years old. Kathy and her late husband, Randy, published a poetry book together which was released after Christmas of 2024. Kathy published a children's book called "Max and the Fire Engine Incident" which was released in August of 2025 and written for pre-school and elementary school age children. This book is written for ages 12 to 19 and is meant to be both entertaining and educational. The books are available on Citi of Books, Barnes and Noble and Christian Publishers web sites. Kathy strives to make reading both entertaining, enjoyable and educational for the children of the world.

Kathy has an Associate's Degree in Computer Information Systems from Harford Community College located in Bel Air, Maryland and a double major Bachelor's degree in Business and CIS from the College of Notre Dame of Maryland located in Baltimore, Maryland. She graduated with Phi Theta Kappa and Cum Laude honors.

Max
Max

About the main character, Max

In this story, Max portrays the supreme leader as commander. He plans and organizes strategies to defeat Hisler, the Bulldog tyrant. He cares about his generals and men. The quality of life for every dog is of paramount importance to him. He is strong and brave in his pursuit of justice, equality and freedom for all dogs. Max is a great example of leadership for all dogs and becomes a war hero

MAX, the Scotch Commander Poem

Max 's generals, he likes to meet

The Great Dane, Wire-Haired Terrier and Grey Hound he greets

He rewards them with treats

He makes sure they have warm housing, plenty of food and the like

They are all in excellent shape and in good sight

His is brave and loyal to his men as can be

Max is very well liked and a real leader you see

No matter how large the mount, MAX will stand his ground

The men carry out his orders, no one makes a sound

Heisler is no match for MAX

And that is a fact!

Max and his generals will carry on with all their might

To the end, they will fight

They will defeat Heisler and that will be a pretty sight!

ADVENTURES OF
MAX
THE SCOTCH COMMANDER
KATHY RUTH (HALL) HAACK

Kathy, Jamie and Max
at the Culpeper airport

INTRODUCTION

3

Hello, my name is Maximillian, but my friends and family call me Max. I'm a Scotch terrier by birth, and I live with my mother in Dumfries, Virginia. I took flying lessons in Culpeper, Virginia with my cousin, Jamie. I want to tell you about an adventure I had in my younger days when they called me Max, the Scotch commander.

Jamie's brother Brody, lives in Spean Bridge, Scotland where the three Marine World War II statues overlook the harbor. Jamie and I flew over to visit him in my WWII Boeing Stearing airplane. Brody told us about the terrible tyrant Bulldog called Hesler, who was conquering Scotland and surrounding countries. Brody was a member of the resistance, and they found Hesler's war plan. The resistance worked underground in Portsmouth, England where the dock yard had many war ships and ferries that frequented the harbor. Brody was warning us that Hesler's plan was to eventually conquer the United States.

HEISLER'S PSYCHOLOGY, BACKGROUND AND PLAN

Heisler thought Bulldogs were the supreme dog race and should rule the world. He lived in Germany and he became a very popular leader with a great army of Gray and brown Bulldogs. He conquered the surrounding countries of Italy, France to the South, Demark, Norway, and Finland to the north. Only Bulldogs were allowed to join his army and all other breeds of dogs like Poodles, Scotch terriers, Greyhounds, Collies and all others were his slave dogs. They lived in a huge dog factory where they had to produce the metal bone weapons used in war and the engineer bulldogs built the submarines and tanks needed for war. The Bulldogs trained in the rouged terrain of Spean Bridge in the Scottish Highlands.

The Royal Scotsman Train

Heisler decided that he would invade Washington and eventually rule all American dogs. His plan was to travel by the Royal Scotsman Train with his army to the harbor where they would board a special submarine to cross the Atlantic Ocean. This submarine had a bulldog face on the front and would lead the land attack at the Dumfries Port in Virginia located on the Potomac River off the Chesapeake Bay.

MAX'S PLAN

I organized a huge army of every breed of dog who wanted to enlist. From the north came friends and family from Baltimore, Perry Hall, and Jarrettsville in MD who volunteered. Many volunteers came from Pennsylvania, Dumfries, Woodbridge, and Manassas in Virginia. Also, their friends from West Virginia, North and South Carolina came. The Army Base was in Quantico, Virginia near my home in Dumfries, Virginia.

I was the chief and commander of this entire American dog army. They called me Max, the Scotch Commander. The general of my army was Eisenach, the Great Dane. The dog tank specialist was Lieutenant Patrick, the determined Wired Hair terrier. My Navy general was Schwartz, the notorious Greyhound. They were all trained in weaponry and war tactics at Quantico. I posted watchmen at the Dumfries Port looking for the Bulldog submarine where we had hidden bunkers 24 hours a day. The bunkers contained food, shelter and sleeping quarters for my dogs with excellent communication devices. Under my orders, General Schwartz commanded 10 Scotti submarines guarding the length of the shoreline surrounding Port Dumfries. General Eisenach with the army and Lieutenant Patrick with 10 Scotti dog tanks waited in secret behind the bunkers ready for any intimate attack.

RF D MJ627
SPITFIRE
MAX

THE WAR BEGINS

Heisler was in the local papers in occupied Paris, France where the girls did the can-can dance for the German Bulldogs in local restaurants. In Calis, France, the Germans were in the hospital getting medical treatment. Poland was occupied near Warsaw. Some of the Bulldogs were fighting in Dublin and Poland with tanks and trucks to the east.

Heisler divided his army. Half of his army traveled by ship down the Rhine to reach the English Channel, then to reach London, England where they met colleagues at the Orchard Pub for drinks and dog treats before the land attack.

Then they fiercely and furiously attacked by land. However, the British had a surprise for them and while they embarked on British soil, the British super marine Spit fire WWII fighter plane designed by Reginal Joseph Mitchell in 1936 attacked the Bulldogs on the shores. The Spit fire was a streamlined aircraft and had a very smooth take off giving them an edge in the frontal attack. The Germans painted their aircraft colors of red, green, blue and brown. The English bombed the Germans camp of the planes of many colors and destroyed most of the aircraft which was about twenty planes, supplies, the mess hall and barracks. The Germans acquired new planes and hit the British camp, destroying planes, buildings, medical personnel and pilots.

The Polish Airforce joined in to help the British Airforce, 303 squadron defeat the Bulldogs. During the battle of Britain, the Polish squadron shot down 126 enemy aircraft losing only eight pilots and bravely cheered "Long live King George". The Spit fire planes were instrumental in winning the war. Unfortunately, Mitchell did not live to see his planes used in WWII as he died in 1937.

THE POTOMAC ENCOUNTER: GREYHOUND VS. GERMAN U-BOATS

Meanwhile, Heisler crossed the Atlantic in his Bulldog submarines in the dead of the night hoping to surprise our army coming up the Potomac River. General Schwartz, my navy Greyhound under my orders, torpedoed most of the Bulldog subs in the debts of the Potomac River and destroyed most of Heisler's navy. Heisler's private Bull dog sub reached Port Dumfries. I lead the land attack with General Eisenach, the Great Dane.

THE WAR ENDS AND HEISLER IS DEFEATED

Under my command, Lieutenant Patrick, my victorious wired-haired terrier with his 10 Scottie dog tanks, assaulted Heisler and his remaining army. There were many Bulldog causalities and Heisler was wounded from dog bone shrapnel.

I took Heisler and the remaining Bull dogs back to Germany to stand trial for their war crimes. The fierce Heisler Bulldog and his loyal bulldogs stood trial in Nuremburg, Germany. There were hundreds of witnesses. The trial took two weeks as there were hundreds of witnesses that testified in court against Heisler. Heisler was convicted of cruelty of the bulldogs he imprisoned and war crimes and sentenced to a life term never to be paroled. He would have a diet of bread and water with no treats forever. His loyal followers were each sentenced to a 40-year prison term.

VICTORY AND PEACE

All dogs in the United States, Europe, England, Germany, France, Poland and surrounding lands now have freedom, security, justice and peace. The dogs taken by Heisler as slaves in his prisons were medically treated and released to their families. They were awarded damages of $100,000 each by the court.

There were world celebrations with fireworks displays and parties with all kinds of dog treats in honor of all dog breeds. Peace, harmony and happiness once again reigned upon the earth. It was like dog heaven!

This story contained some true historical facts, a lot of action and important concepts like justice, equality, freedom, honor, bravery, hope and faith that were illustrated.

Max and I hope you enjoyed the story and will read more of Max's adventures in the future.

Love,

Max and Kathy

THE END

19

Facts or Fiction

Fact

Max is a real Scotch Terrier who lives in Dumfries, Virginia with the Author.

Jamie is a real person who is the author's grandson.

Jamie does frequent Culpeper airport and does take flying lessons in Manassas, Virginia.

Brody is a real person and is the Author's grandson but lives in Woodbridge, Virginia.

Reginald Joseph Mitchell did design the WWII Spit Fire airplane in 1936.

Mitchell did die in 1937 before his Spit Fire airplane was used in the actual WWII battle.

The Spit Fire airplanes were instrumental in winning the Battle of Britain.

The various breeds portrayed in the story are true breeds.

The Royal Marine Commandos Statue located in the Scotland highlands is real.

The Spean Bridge in the Scottish Highlands is a true location that was used in this story.

The Spean Bridge location was used in WWII for a six-week training course for soldiers and is still being used today.

The Royal Scotsman Train is a real train operating in Scotland today.

The Polish Squadron 303 did help the British defeat the Germans in the actual WWII battle.

The Germans did paint their war planes the various colors mentioned in the actual WWII battle.

Hitler (not Hisler of course) was in the newspapers in occupied Paris, France and the girls did do the can- can for the German soldiers (not the Bulldogs) in the local restaurants.

Fiction

The story itself is fictitious and created by the author.

Historical Pictures

Building of the railroad for the now-famous
Royal Scotsman train

WWII Tanks

Max's Pictures

Max in Stary Night

by: Kathy Ruth (Hall) Haack

www.ingramcontent.com/pod-product-compliance
Lightning Source LLC
Chambersburg PA
CBRC090744110726
48005CB00007B/969